This book belongs to

❄ _____ ❄

This is a Parragon book
This edition published in 2006

Parragon
Queen Street House
4 Queen Street
BATH, BA1 1HE, UK

ISBN 1-40545-036-3

Printed in China

Little Ice Skater

Written by Gaby Goldsack

Illustrated by Caroline Jayne Church

p

Grace glided across the ice, spun on her toes, then slid to a halt beside the rest of the class. Grace was the youngest pupil in the class, but she was already skating better than most of them.

"Well done, Grace. Well done, everyone," smiled Mrs Hobbs, the teacher. "Now don't forget that we're holding auditions for parts in *Swan Lake* next week."

Grace's eyes lit up. *Swan Lake* was a lovely story. It was all about a princess called Odette, who was turned into a swan by a wicked magician. Each night Odette became human for a few hours, and one night she fell in love with Prince Siegfried. Downley Academy of Ice-Skating was going to perform it on ice, and Grace's mum had promised to take her to the auditions.

On the day of the auditions,
Grace and her mum arrived
at the ice rink early.

"You're bound to get a part,"
said Grace's mum.

But Grace wasn't so sure. The other
girls and boys were all so much older
than she was.

Grace watched Felicity Keevil
glide gracefully across the ice
on one leg.

"I wish I could skate like that," she
sighed.

"But you can," said her mum,
giving her a quick hug.

"MUM!" said Grace, rolling her eyes and smiling. Felicity Keevil was Downley Academy's star pupil. There was no way Grace would ever skate as well as Felicity.

By the time it was Grace's turn to skate she was a bundle of nerves. Her tummy fluttered with butterflies and her knees felt like jelly. She was sure that she was going to make a fool of herself.

But as the music began to play, everything changed. She forgot about everyone else and skated brilliantly.

"Lovely," said Mrs Hobbs. But Grace still didn't expect to get a part. She clapped her hands as Felicity Keevil was given the part of Odette. Then she blinked in surprise as she was told that she was to be Felicity's understudy. "That means, that if Felicity falls ill or anything, you have to play Odette," explained her mum.

Grace took her role as understudy very seriously. She practiced alongside Felicity whenever she could, following her around the rink like a little shadow. And when Felicity wasn't around, Grace practiced alone. She also made sure that her mum took her along to every rehearsal. Together they watched Felicity and the rest of the cast glide through their routines.

Grace thought Felicity was wonderful.

"She skates like a real princess," she told her mum.

"She's going to be perfect as Odette. I hope nothing happens to her. I know I wouldn't be half as good."

After weeks and weeks of practice, the day of the dress rehearsal arrived. The ice rink was full of laughter and chatter as all the girls and boys glided around in their splendid costumes.

Grace couldn't help feeling just the teeniest bit left out as she watched Felicity and the other girls skate around dressed as beautiful swans. She imagined she was out there with them.

"One day that will be me," she thought. Then she sat back to watch Felicity skate her way through the last act.

When Felicity made her final spin, Grace sat forward and got ready to clap. But as Felicity landed, her blades wobbled and she fell to the ground with a thud.

"Oh, no," gasped Grace, leaping to her feet.

"Are you okay?" Mrs Hobbs asked Felicity.

"Yes, I think so," replied Felicity. But when she tried to walk, she let out a yelp. "Ouch," she cried. "I think I've twisted my ankle." Mrs Hobbs felt Felicity's ankle, then shook her head.

"It's not too bad but you'll have to rest it for a couple of days. I don't think you'll be able to skate on the opening night."

"But what will we do?" asked Jake, the boy who was playing Prince Siegfried. "We can't perform *Swan Lake* without Odette." A hush fell over the ice rink. Everyone knew he was right. They would have to cancel the show.

"But what about Grace?" asked Felicity, breaking the silence. "She's my understudy and knows the part better than I do."

All eyes turned on Grace. Grace did her best to hide behind her mum.

"Yes, what about it?" asked Mrs Hobbs. "Will you do it?"

Grace gulped nervously and wished that the ground would swallow her up. There was no way that she could play Odette. But on the other hand, she couldn't let everyone down. She took a deep breath, counted to ten, and then nodded her head.

Everyone let out a sigh of relief. The show would go on!

That night, after she had gone to bed, Grace tossed and turned beneath her covers. Silly thoughts whirled through her head. What would happen if she forgot her steps? What would happen if she tripped and fell? What would happen if everyone thought she was rubbish? It was no good. There was no way she could sleep.

Grace climbed out of bed
and went over to the window.
Stars twinkled in the
moonlit sky. Suddenly,
something caught Grace's eye.
It was a shooting star.
Quickly, Grace made a wish.
"I wish I had something that
would make me feel more
confident. Something that
would help me skate as
gracefully as Felicity."
Then, feeling suddenly tired,
Grace fell into bed.
Within seconds, she was
fast asleep.

On the night of the opening performance, Grace sat quietly in a corner of the changing room as the other boys and girls got ready. She looked down at her beautiful costume and sighed. She might look like a star but she certainly didn't feel like one.

"Five minutes until the opening act," called Mrs Hobbs. The other boys and girls thundered out of the changing room.

Grace tried to stand up but her legs weren't working. They felt worse than jelly. Her eyes prickled with tears.

"I can't do it," she thought. "I can't play Odette. I'm going to let everyone down."

Suddenly, Grace's mum popped her head around the changing room door. "I've got a visitor for you," she announced. Grace blinked back her tears as Felicity limped into the room.

Felicity took one look at Grace's pale face and flopped down beside her. "I've come to wish you good luck," she smiled.

Grace's lips wobbled and words gushed out of her mouth. "I can't go out there and skate in front of all those people," she told Felicity. "It's no good. Look, I'm shaking with nerves. I can't even stand up."

Felicity put her arm around the smaller girl.

"Shall I let you into a little secret?" she whispered. "I used to get really nervous. You should have seen me. My knees would knock together and my feet wouldn't do as they were told. But then my mum gave me this." She reached around her neck to show Grace a shiny pendant.

When Grace looked more closely, she saw
that it was a tiny silver ice-skating boot.

"It's a lucky charm," explained Felicity.
"When I'm wearing this I know that everything's
going to be all right. And look," she added,
pulling something out of her pocket.
"I've got one for you."

As Felicity fastened the charm around her
neck, Grace smiled for the
first time that evening.
Her fears began to
melt away and she
began to feel
excited.

A few tiny butterflies still fluttered in Grace's tummy as she slid onto the ice. But as soon as the music began they disappeared completely.

When Grace was dressed as Princess Odette, she danced like a real princess. And when she was dressed as a swan, she danced like a swan.

In what seemed to Grace like no time at all, the performance came to an end. As she made her final curtsy, the rink erupted with applause. Grace beamed with delight. She'd done it.

Grace glanced around the rink until she saw Felicity.
She was standing next to Grace's mum,
clapping harder than anyone else was.

"Thank you," mouthed Grace.
"Thank you for my lovely lucky charm."